Sherlock Holmes
The Man with the Twisted Script

Sherlock Holmes illustrations for the modern day

Michael J. Foy

Paperback ISBN 978-1-78705-843-9

Published by MX Publishing
335 Princess Park Manor, Royal Drive,
London, N11 3GX
www.mxpublishing.com

Cover design by Brian Belanger.

Other Books by the Same Author

The Curious Book of Sherlock Holmes Characters.

Sherlock Holmes – A Study in Illustrations Vol 1.

Foreword

So we survived 2020 with most of our sanity intact. My wife and I visited England last Christmas and it wasn't very enjoyable, 10 days of quarantine and then put into Tier 4 lockdown, we nearly lost it, and we only had to put up for it for 21 days before returning to USA, how the rest of you survived I just don't know, So I say well done, maybe humour helped, so to that end, here is a funny (Hopefully) book to cheer everybody up and maybe give you a smile or two.

Years ago, many, many years ago, I managed to win one of Punch's if the Caption fits competition (it is actually included in their book 'If the Caption Fits…. Page whatever!) so while I was preparing the book 'Sherlock Holmes – A Study in Illustrations', I had to look at Thousands of images from various illustrators and since Volume 1 is mainly about Sidney Paget and all of his Sherlock Holmes drawings, I had to chuckle at one or two of them, so I posted the Hall Pycroft shirt one on Facebook and a few people liked it, which made me wonder if I there were other images that I could pummel into submission and mangle about. Hence this book. I hope you like it, please take special note of the Hugh Boone illustration ☺

All the best and keep safe in 2021

Michael Foy, back in Florida 2021 (at last)

The king of Bohemia clearly hasn't quite worked out the mandatory Covid mask wearing.

Well Holmes, it looks like you have 4 numbers and the Bonus ball, we have enough for a take-out.

Group Shot – A Scandal in Bohemia

"Well I don't think I brought that in on my shoe!"

"I wonder if I can interest you in a donation to the new Church Roof."

"So for a good selfie, you stand like this with your smartphone in your left hand. Don't forget to pucker your lips!"

Group Shot – A Scandal in Bohemia

"Not another copy of that stupid Sherlock Holmes Caption book!"

Jabez Wilson from The Red-Headed League.

"My Horoscope says 'Expect a large bill for the repair of your Cellar', how very strange."

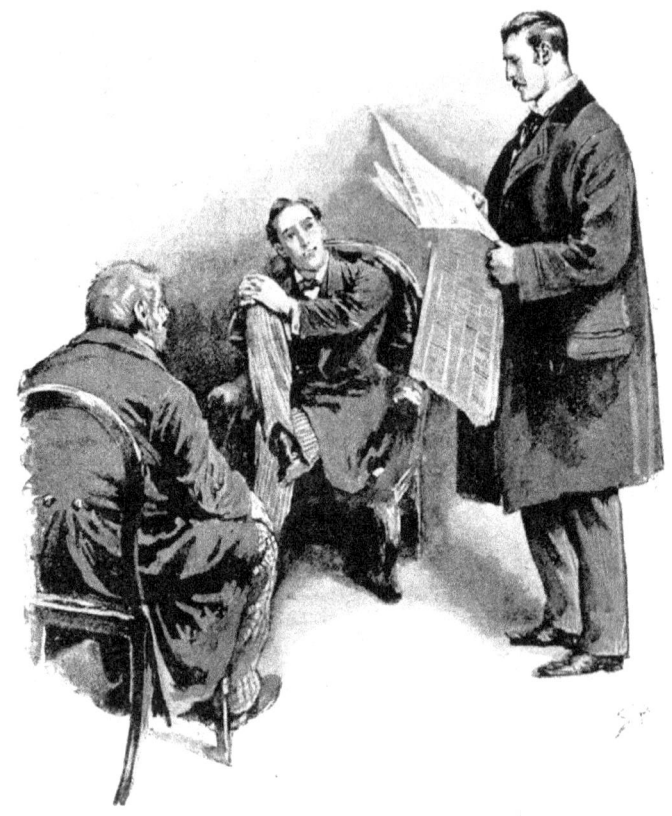

"I agree, this Sudoku is particularly difficult."

"Oh Bother, 'You must wear a mask' and I forgot to bring one."

"Now let me think, I'm sure that arm chair corner was in the IKEA pack."

"Excuse me sirs, do you know who stole my front door?"

"Tag! You're it, now catch me!"

"Let me just steady myself on this table, Hic! I had a few too many Gins at lunchtime. Hic!"

"Let me show you the rest of my 50 Shades of Grey equipment."

"So Holmes, are you Stalking a Deer today?"

"I don't know how anyone can possibly sit on that chair without falling through the back either."

"..and I had to stand all the way on the Underground"

"Oh No!, Rover from the Prisoner TV show has found me"

"I'm so glad I upgraded to these new LED lanterns."

Outside Hugh Boone's cell – The man with the Twisted Lip

I don't see why he can't get to sleep without his SpongeBob SquarePants doll."

"I'm sorry Holmes I don't think this is going to fool Col. Sebastian Moran."

"So I have to put all those adverts into the papers and even get another goose and this is all you give me?"

Holmes lights a cigarette - Copper Beeches

"I don't think that 'pocket lighter' is going to sell, who has 2-foot-long pockets?"

Violet Hunter – Copper Beeches

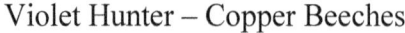

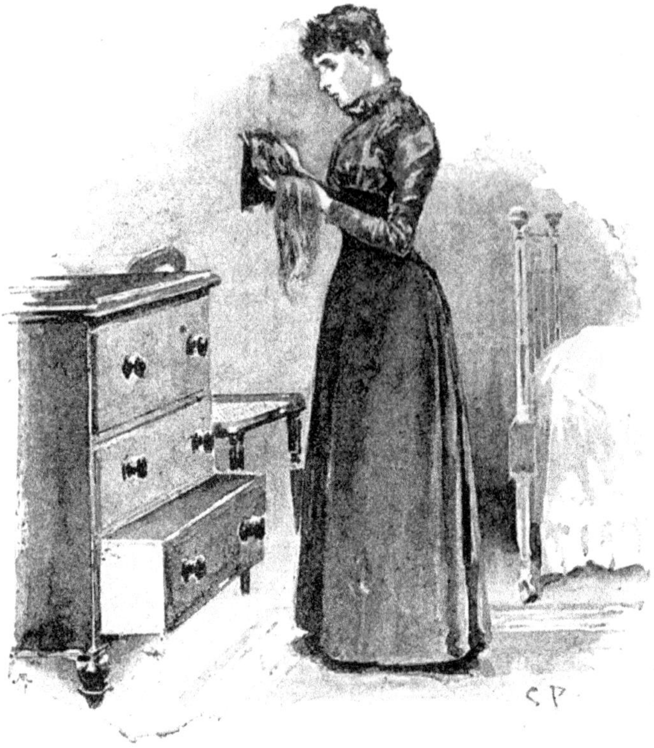

“I really must stop collecting my belly button fluff.”

"Perhaps you can find the pea, with only two shells."

"When I call your rental boat number – You come in. Understand?"

Mr. & Mrs. Munro – The adventure of Yellow Face

"I'm sorry dear, I'm putting my foot down – No more Bake-off"

"8..9..10., here we come ready or not."

Hall Pycroft complains to Holmes about the amount of starch in his shirt sleeves.

Group – The Stockbroker's Clerk

"Ignore him in the corner, he's just sulking because we didn't bring enough chairs.

"So there I was, asleep in the park and this duck walked all over me."

"Well it looks like someone scratched 'SP' on the stones."

Mycroft Holmes – The Greek Interpreter

"I don't know, it smells like a fart to me."

"I agree, it is a rather small Television."

"Let's face it Paul, you are better off using an electric razor."

SP

"Wow, I'd give that toilet a couple of minutes, If I were you!"

In the Reichenbach Diving competition, as Holmes and Moriarty fight over who is going to wear the swimming hat, they drop it and so the answer is neither of them.

"We are only meant to bring along one 23kg suitcase each, Watson."

"OK, you can come in, but the horse stays outside."

"I can never find my reading glasses when I need them."

"Well sonny, you can have this Toblerone, if you deliver a message for me."

"Oh, Henry, You've been eating Garlic again, haven't you?"

"Am I too late for breakfast?"

Major set-back as new driverless carriage drives off
without a passenger.

"We caught her officers, wearing a mask that didn't cover her nose."

Problems at a fancy-dress party when two men come dressed as Batman.

"I see you came straight from your Beekeeping job."

Holmes gets caught playing Knock, Knock, Ginger

H & W – Abbey Grange

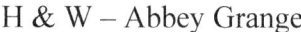

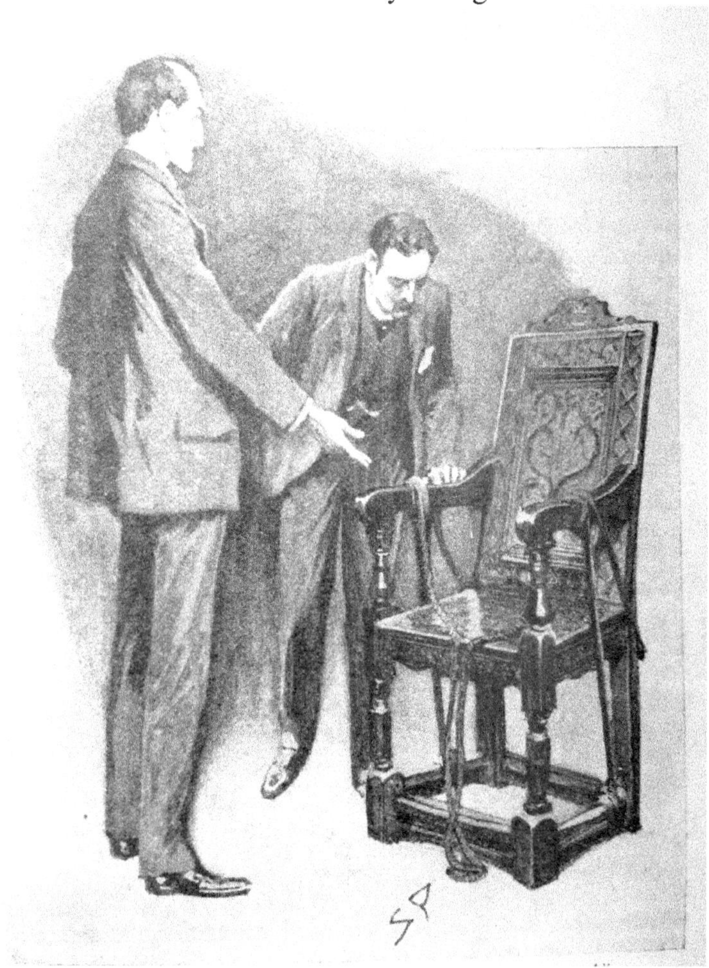

"This should spice up our Wednesday evenings."

"Watson, did you remember to bring some bread?"

"Do you like my new Asbestos Trousers- good to 5000°c

"Did you know the putty has fallen out on this window."

"You arrived late, so you get the uncomfortable chair."

"Wow, this meal costs a packet, let's go Dutch."

"Please Help, I'm a struggling Sherlock Holmes Author.

"And for my next trick, I shall make my thumb disappear!"

"On three, we jump out and shout Happy Birthday!"

"This is the last time, Watson, that I get your football out of the mire!

"I agree with you, Gentleman, this wallpaper doesn't look
like it's worth £840 a roll, no matter what Boris says."

Lord Robert St. Simon – The Nobel Bachelor

"And for my next trick, I shall pull a rabbit from my hat."

Lestrade with H & W – The Nobel bachelor

"Bag for life Rubbish! I've had it two weeks and the bottom's split."

"Hatty, come quickly, Primark are doing a two-for one sale."

"I've come to get my football that's stuck on your wall."

Whispered behind bowler :"I've heard she's a right little raver!"

Even after the boat sank, people in steerage were treated poorly.

"For God's sake, don't go in that Bar – They have a Karaoke machine set up.

When the game of Twister, gets a bit rough!

"Watch it ladies, there's some quick-sand here."

Percy Trevelyan and patient - The Resident Patient

SP

"Thank you for bringing in this chair today and I have to say that it is certainly older and in better condition than you."

"Of course you can have the last Spring Roll, Percy."

"Watch it Holmes, Sidney Paget didn't draw that bit."

"Hurry up Holmes, we don't want to get caught letting these tyres down.

Lestrade, Holmes & Watson – The Six Napoleons

"They say they will be fitting a 'Sherlock Holmes lived here' Blue Plaque right there.

And now a quick word from our sponsors

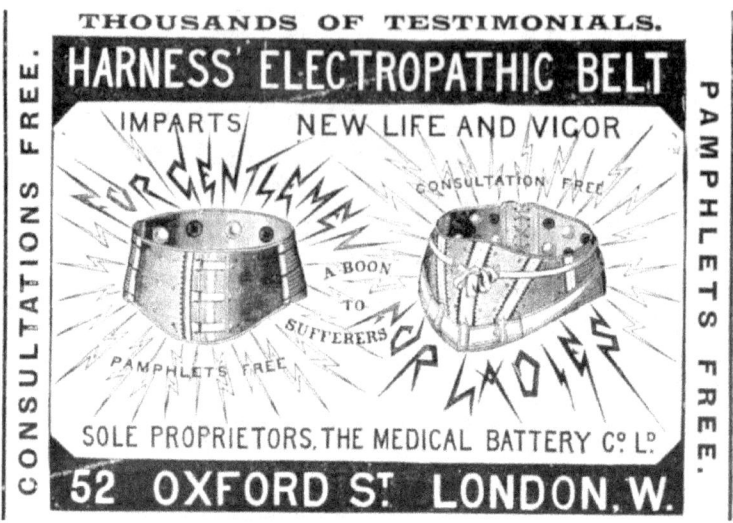

Personally I don't want this belt anywhere near my
Testimonials

Sir Arthur Conan Doyle's Sherlock Holmes titles, ruined by adding an extra word

A Study in Scarlet *O'Hara*
The Sign of Four *Horsemen*
A Scandal in Bohemia *Rhapsody*
The red-headed *Football* League
A *Suit* Case of Identity
The Boscombe *Chad* Valley Mystery
The Five Orange *Greenwich* Pips
The Man with the Twisted Lip-*Stick*
The Blue Carbuncle *Lanced*
The Speckled Band-*Aid*
The Engineer's Thumb *nail*
The Noble *Gas* Bachelor
Beryl *Reid* Coronet
Copper *Nude*-Beeches
Silver Blaze Extinguished
The Cardboard Box *Kitten*
The Yellow *Clown* Face
The *Nude* Stockbroker's Clerk
The Gloria Scott *sings*
The Musgrave Ritual *Dancing*
The Reigate *Alright!* Squire
The *Straight* Crooked Man
The Resident *Out*-Patient
The Greek *Salad* Interpreter
The Naval *Gazing* Treaty
The Final *Sudoku* Problem
The *News*-Hound of the Baskervilles
The Empty House *Party*
The Norwood *Body* Builder

The *Morris* **Dancing Men**
The Solitary *uni*-**Cyclist**
The Priory School *Inspector*
Black *Pudding* **Peter**
Charles Augustus Milverton *Juggler*
Six Napoleons, *Bartender*
Three Students *Loans*
Golden Pince-Nez *Binoculars*
Not **Missing Three-Quarter**
Downton **Abbey Grange**
The Second *wine* **Stain**
Wisteria *Beaver* **Lodge**
Bruce-Partington *Floor* **Plans**
Devil's Foot *pump*
The Red Circle *Line*
Lady Frances Carfax *Report*
Tie-**Dying Detective**
The *Frankie* **Valley of Fear**
His Last Bow-icon*Tie*.
Mazarin *Gall* **Stone**
Thor Bridge *Game*
The Creeping *Damp* **Man**
Sussex Vampire *Bat*
Three Garridebs *Tap*
The Illustrious Client *Strips*
The Three *Clark* **Gables**
The Blanched *Almonds* **Soldier**
The Lion's Mane *Haircut*
The Retired Colourman *Pallette*
Seven **Veiled Lodger**
Shoscombe Old *Fire*-**Place**

Also from Mike Foy

Imagine the scene, 221b baker street, Sherlock Holmes and Dr. John Watson are in their rooms, Holmes is smoking his pipe staring at the ceiling,

"Watson he cries, What do you know about Vanderbilt? Make a long arm and look in that wonderful book 'The Curious Book of Sherlock Holmes Characters', a truly remarkable work, packed will information about every character we have encountered in our 56 short stories and 4 novellas. This writer has even included that carbuncle eating goose and that lazy dog that did nothing."

Watson stretched out his arm and picked it up from the coffee table, "I like to keep it handy, it looks so nice on this table, giving the whole room an air of sophistication. In addition it's so large and thick, it would stop an air rifle bullet at a thousand yards. Only the other day I looked up Captain Calhoun and Messrs. Biddle, Hayward and Moffat and found that there was a link between these individuals."

Holmes thought a moment, and said "What links Miss Hunter, Miss Smith, Miss Westbury and Miss De Merville?", "Too easy" cried Watson. "What about this Holmes, get those braincells working, Which Canon story has 4 totally unrelated people with the same surname (last name), I can give you a clue, one was a policeman, one was an alias, one was a teen and one was an official. "

"And this book lists them all?" asked Holmes,

"Yes, there are over one thousand characters in it and of course, we both get a special mention, and it's illustrated throughout"

"Sidney Paget again, I suppose?"

"Oh no, not just him, but artists like Frederic Dorr Steele of Collier's fame, Ernest Flammarion, F. H. Townsend, Josef Friedrich, Paul Thiriat, Richard Gutschmidt, Arthur Twidle et al. It's a must have for anyone seriously into Us."

Mike Foy's mammoth book includes all the characters (animals included) from the Sherlock Holmes canon, with as many illustrations as possible. It's one of the largest compilations of its kind and an excellent reference resource for Sherlock Holmes fans.

Also from Mike Foy

Sherlock Holmes is truly a 'Man for All Seasons' and his image has been worked and re-worked for over a century. Unsurprisingly the illustrated Holmes of 1887 differs from that of today. In this multi-volume work, we will show how various illustrators have visualised Holmes and other characters who appeared in Arthur Conan Doyle's works. Later volumes will celebrate Holmes in non-Canonical stories as illustrators and authors placed Holmes in fresh adventures, but more of that later.

This volume is not going to be diverse; it is true to say that one person dominates. While it is true that there are illustrations by Charles Altamont Doyle, David Henry Friston, James Grieg, and Walter Stanley Paget - the majority of this book is dominated by one person - Sidney Paget.